# LA CORONA
## AND THE TIN FROG

RUSSELL HOBAN
AND NICOLA BAYLEY

JONATHAN CAPE
THIRTY BEDFORD SQUARE LONDON

*For my children*  R. H.

*For my parents*  N. B.

First published 1979
Text © 1974 by Russell Hoban
Illustrations © 1979 by Nicola Bayley
Jonathan Cape Ltd, 30 Bedford Square, London WC1

These tales first appeared in *Puffin Annual 1974*

British Library Cataloguing in Publication Data
Hoban, Russell
La Corona and the tin frog, and other tales.
I. Title   II. Bayley, Nicola
823'.9'1J     PZ7.H637
ISBN 0–224–01397–1

Printed in Italy by A. Mondadori Editore, Verona

## La Corona and the Tin Frog

L A Corona was the name of the beautiful lady in the picture on the inside of the cigar box lid. She wore a scarlet robe and a golden crown. Beyond her was a calm blue bay on which a paddle-wheel steamer floated. A locomotive trailed a faint plume of smoke across the pink and distant plain past shadowy palms and pyramids. Far off in the printed sky sailed a balloon.

But the lady never looked at any of those things. She sat among wheels and anvils, sheaves of wheat, hammers, toppled pedestals and garden urns, and she pointed to a globe that stood beside her while she looked steadfastly out past the left-hand side of the picture.

Inside the cigar box lived a tin frog, a seashell, a yellow cloth tape measure, and a magnifying glass. The tin frog was bright green and yellow, with two perfectly round eyes that were like yellow-and-black bullseyes. He had cost five shillings when new and hopped when wound up. He had fallen in love with La Corona, and he was wound up all the time because of it. He kept trying to hop into the picture with her, but he only bumped his nose against it and fell back into the box.

"I love you," he told her. But she said nothing, didn't even look at him.

"For heaven's sake!" said the tin frog. "Look at me, won't you! What do you expect to see out there beyond the left-hand side of the picture?"

"Perhaps a handsome prince," said La Corona.

"Maybe I'm a handsome prince," said the tin frog. "You know, an enchanted one."

"Not likely," said La Corona. "You're not even a very handsome frog."

"How do you know if you won't look?" said the tin frog. Again he tried to hop into the picture, and again he only bumped his nose and fell back. "O misery!" he said. "O desperation!"

"Pay close attention," said the magnifying glass.

"To what?" said the tin frog.

"Everything," said the magnifying glass. He leaned up against the picture, and the tin frog looked through him. When he looked very close he saw that the picture was made of coloured printed dots. Looking even closer he saw spaces between the dots.

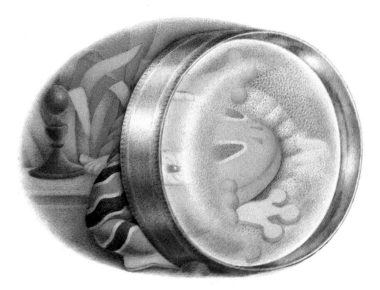

"One doesn't always jump into a picture from the front," said the magnifying glass.

"Do it by the inch," said the tape measure.

"Be deep," said the seashell.

The tin frog thought long and hard. He waited for the moment just between midnight and the twelve strokes of the clock. Everything was dark.

The tin frog dropped the seashell over the side of the cigar box. He heard a splash. "Very good," he said. He unrolled the tape measure over the side of the cigar box. Then he hopped, and found himself in the ocean.

Down, down, down he followed the yellow tape measure in the green and glimmering midnight water. Through coral and sea fans and waving green seaweed he swam, past sunken wrecks and treasures and gliding monsters of the deep, until the tape measure curved up again. Up and up went the tin frog, toward the light, and he came out between the coloured dots of the calm blue bay where the paddle-wheel steamer floated. The dots closed up behind him, and he was in the picture with La Corona.

"Here I am," said the tin frog when he had swum ashore. "I love you."

"You look quite different," said La Corona. "You may not be an enchanted prince, but you *are* an enchanting frog."

They were married soon after that. They took a sea voyage in the paddle-wheel steamer. They drifted far and high across the blue sky in the wicker basket of the balloon. And often they travelled past shadowy palms and pyramids in the train pulled by the locomotive that trailed its faint plume of smoke across the pink and distant plain.

When next the cigar box was opened it was empty. In the picture on the lid La Corona and the tin frog smiled at each other. And among the wheels and anvils, sheaves of wheat and hammers were the magnifying glass, the tape measure, and the seashell.

## The Tin Horseman

THE weather castle was printed on a card that hung by the window. It stood on a rocky island in the middle of a bright blue sea with banners flying from the tops of its tall towers. When the weather was fair the rocky island was blue. When rain threatened the island turned purple, and when the rain fell the island was pink.

The tin horseman lived on a shelf near the window. He had a pale heroic face. He wore a yellow fringed Indian suit and a headdress of red feathers. His dapple-grey horse had a red saddle-cloth. Horse and horseman were a single piece of tin stamped from a mould. They were printed on one side only, the other side was blank. But they were rounded and not flat, and they had feelings.

Long ago there had been a flat tin clown, a red-painted magnet, and two or three coloured rings with the horseman. Now he was alone. Day after day he looked at the little windows of the weather castle, and he was certain that he had seen the face of a beautiful yellow-haired princess at one of them.

"One midnight when the island is blue
I shall gallop there and find her,"
he said. But when the island
was blue he did not gallop
to the castle, because
he was afraid.

The tin horseman was afraid of the round red-and-yellow glass-topped box that was the monkey game of skill. Inside it crouched the monkey, printed on a yellow background. He had a horrid pink face, and empty holes where his eyes belonged. His eyes were silver balls that had to be shaken into place.

The tin horseman was afraid that when the monkey had his eyes in place he might do dreadful things, and he was sure that the monkey was skilful enough to shake them into place whenever he wanted to. The monkey lived between the tin horseman and the castle, and the tin horseman never dared to gallop past.

Day after day he looked at the castle windows, and daily he became more certain that he saw the yellow-haired princess. Once he thought she even waved her hand to him. "When the island is pink I shall gallop there," he said. "One rainy midnight I shall smash the glass and throw away the monkey's silver eyes and ride to the princess." But he was afraid, and stayed where he was, dusty on the shelf.

One night, just between midnight and the twelve strokes of the clock, words came to the tin horseman: "Now or never." He didn't know whether he had heard them or thought them, but his fear left him, and in the dim light from the window he spurred his horse toward the weather castle and the princess of his dream.

Just as he was passing the monkey game of skill he was surrounded by complete darkness. All was black, and he could see nothing. Again words came to him:

"Fear is blind, but courage gives me eyes."

And again the tin horseman did not know where the words came from nor why he did what he did next.

He dismounted, and felt in the dark for the monkey game of skill.

He remembered his thought of smashing the glass and throwing away the eyes, but he did not do that. He shook it gently. One, two, he heard the eyes roll into place. He closed his eyes and waited.

A golden glow came from the glass top of the box, and seeing the glow through his closed eyelids he opened his eyes. The monkey was gone. There in the golden light stood the yellow-haired princess he had longed for. She was not in the weather castle, but here before him.

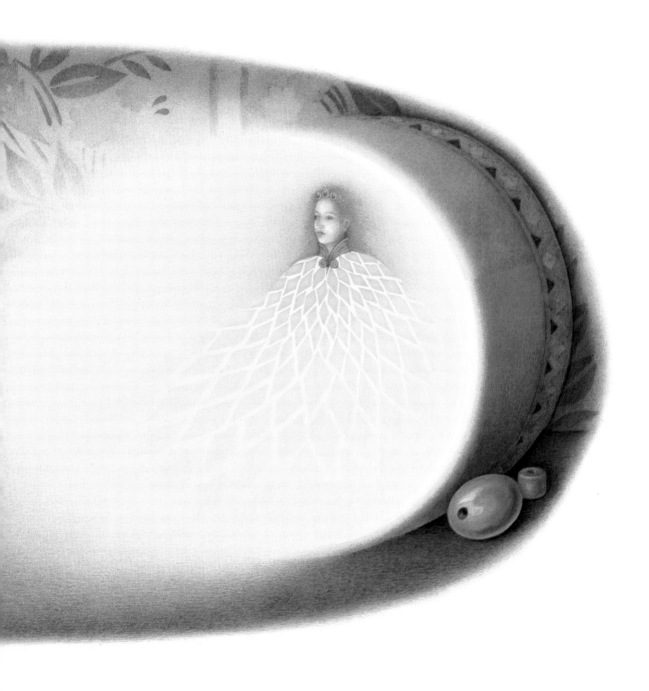

"Your courage has broken my enchantment," she said. "There is a sorcerer who lives in the weather castle. It was he who wanted you to smash the glass and throw away the monkey's eyes, and if you had done that I should have been lost to you for ever."

"Now I *will* ride to the castle," said the tin horseman. He pried the glass top off the box and took the princess up on his horse. Over the blue sea they galloped, straight to the island and up the great stone steps to the castle. The castle was empty. The sorcerer had fled.

After that the tin horseman and the princess lived in the weather castle with the banners flying from the towers, while the island turned blue or pink or purple as the weather changed.

But the glass was back on top of the red-and-yellow box that had been the monkey game of skill. From then on someone else lived there, and no one ever looked to see who it might be.

## The Night Watchman and the Crocodile

HE night watchman was made of wood. He wore a black coat, a top hat and a red kerchief, and he carried a ladder and a long-handled candle snuffer. He was evidently the sort of night watchman who lit and snuffed out the candles in the street lamps and called out the hours in whatever time and place he had come from. His real job was burning incense. His whole hollow body was detachable from the base on which he stood, and when a cone of burning incense was placed on the base and his body put back on top of it the fragrant smoke came out of his open mouth. He called out the hours as well, of course, but no one understood what he was saying. He was totally foreign in speech as well as in appearance, and the clock on the wall could not even recognise the names of the hours called out by the incense-burning wooden night watchman.

The crocodile, tin and handsome, red and green and yellow, rolled on little rubber wheels with a comfortable whirring sound, moving his green legs and opening and closing his splendidly toothed red mouth as he crossed the pattern of the oriental carpet. For years he had said to

himself that he was going to compose a poem for the literary quarterly edited by the spinster mouse who lived behind the skirting board. "I'm definitely going to do it," he said. "It's just a matter of waiting for the right time. It's in me. I have the talent. I have the confidence."

"Half-past ten!" said the night watchman in his own language. He had not understood a word of what the crocodile had said. "Something burns in me," he said. "What is it that burns in me?" No one had explained the incense and its heat and its fragrance to him. It was simply something that happened inside him from time to time. "Such a burning in me!" said the night watchman. "Such a fragrance! I am burning, burning, burning to say something!"

"Of course," said the crocodile, who in his turn understood nothing of what the night watchman said, "for you life is simple. You are secure with your ladder and your candle snuffer. You are not especially burning to say anything; your fragrant smoke is enough for you. You have a working-class outlook, and you are happier because of it."

"Burning to say something!" shouted the night watchman. "It is in me, something to say!"

"You simply don't know how it is with literary people like me," the crocodile went on. "The waiting, waiting, waiting for that perfect time!"

The night watchman had burned more incense than usual that evening. He was giddy with the fragrance and the heat of it, words danced in his head. In all the words of his own language he found nothing to say, but as the hours passed his mind became full of the sounds of the

language the crocodile spoke so flowingly. Unknown words danced in his head. Eleven o'clock came, half-past eleven. Then it was midnight, and there was that tiny buzzing pause while the clock gathered itself to strike twelve times.

"NOW IS THE ONLY TIME THERE IS!" shouted the night watchman. He shouted in the crocodile's language, in words he did not know the meaning of.

"What's that?" said the startled crocodile as the clock finished its twelve strokes.

The night watchman could not say it again. The words had vanished from his mind. His incense had burnt out. But the crocodile had heard him well enough.

"Is it?" said the crocodile. "Is now the only time there is?" He ran back and forth upon the oriental carpet, whirring excitedly. Without

further delay he composed a strong poem, went quickly to the hole in the skirting-board, and recited it to the spinster mouse.

"This is very good indeed," she said. "We'll run it in the next issue. I never thought you'd do it."

"That night watchman is extraordinary," said the crocodile. He ran back across the carpet and stopped in front of the night watchman. "Tell me more," he said. "I feel that I have much to learn from you."

But the night watchman's incense was burnt out. He had forgotten what he had said, and he had never understood the words to begin with. In the evenings that followed he never got hot enough to speak that language again.

The crocodile, however, remembered his words. He went on making poems, and in time there were enough of them to fill a book, which was published by the mouse.

# The Clock

**T**HE clock, ticking and tocking, swinging his pendulum behind the glass front of his case and striking the hours day and night, thought long about the things that had happened in the room. He had seen the tin frog find a way into the picture with La Corona; he had seen the tin horseman break the enchantment of the yellow-haired princess; he had heard the night watchman cry out in words that made the tin crocodile compose poetry. The clock noticed that the crucial moment was always just after his hands touched midnight and just before he sounded his twelve strokes.

He thought about it more and more, and he began to feel left out because he himself could never do anything in that in-between moment except go on keeping time. "Of course," he said to himself, "keeping time is very important. I am sure it's more important than anything those others have done."

He went on ticking and tocking and striking the hours. "All the same," he said to himself, "sometimes I wonder whether I keep time or time keeps me. In a way I'm really no better than a prisoner on a treadmill, walking day and night my tick-tock wheel."

The clock was wound once a week. As the time for each new winding approached he could feel his mainspring losing power. He determined to stop his pendulum, if he could, just at that moment when his hands touched midnight and before he struck the twelve strokes.

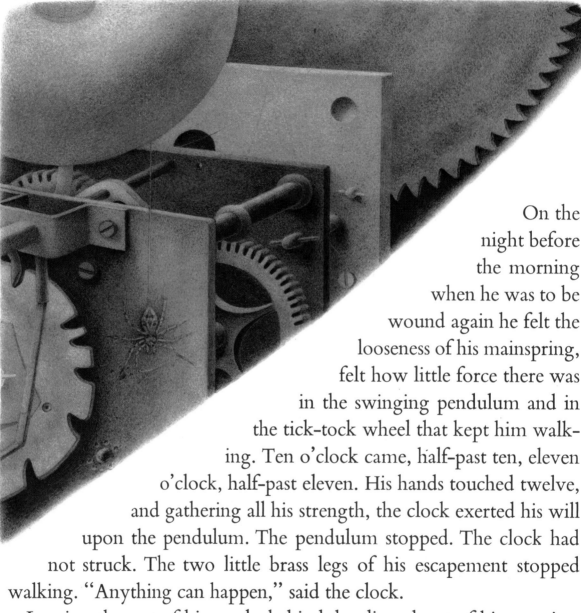

On the
night before
the morning
when he was to be
wound again he felt the
looseness of his mainspring,
felt how little force there was
in the swinging pendulum and in
the tick-tock wheel that kept him walking. Ten o'clock came, half-past ten, eleven
o'clock, half-past eleven. His hands touched twelve,
and gathering all his strength, the clock exerted his will
upon the pendulum. The pendulum stopped. The clock had
not struck. The two little brass legs of his escapement stopped
walking. "Anything can happen," said the clock.

Leaving the rest of his works behind, he slipped out of his case, just
the two little walking brass legs of him, and walked down the wall.

In the picture inside the cigar box lid La Corona and the tin frog
listened for the twelve strokes of midnight, but heard nothing. The
coloured dots of the picture moved apart, moved farther and farther

apart. "Hold me tight," said La Corona to the tin frog. "I am only coloured dots like the rest of the picture."

"No," said the tin frog. "You are no longer only a picture, you are my beloved." He held her tight, and she stayed together as they dropped out of the lid into the cigar box, and the magnifying glass, the seashell, and the tape measure fell with them.

They climbed out of the cigar box, down from the shelf, and stood in the moonlight on the oriental carpet. On the wall the dim hands of the clock stood motionless at mid-night.

On the rocky island on the card by the window the weather castle vanished, and the tin horseman and his princess galloped over the blue sea as it disappeared, then leaped down to the carpet with the others.

The incense-burning night watchman found that he could speak the language of the others. "Now is the only time there is!" was the first thing he said.

The tin crocodile, who had been reading proofs, said, "I haven't even *begun* to make poems yet."

The spinster mouse editor shot out of the hole in the skirting board and said, "Quarterly is not enough!"

"Who's keeping time now?" said the magnifying glass.

"Time can't be kept," said the brass legs of the clock's escapement. "And time can't keep you."

Across the oriental carpet he marched in the moonlight, up the

wall, and stood on the sill of the open window.

As he marched he sang, "Ting-tang, tantarang!"

Everyone followed him across the carpet and up to the window-sill.

"Where will our next castle be, I wonder?" said the yellow-haired princess to the tin horseman.

"What do you suppose the new picture will be?" said La Corona to the tin frog.

"Now!" said the incense-burning night watchman.

"Deep!" said the seashell.

"Thousands and thousands of leagues by the inch!" said the tape measure.

"Pay close attention!" said the magnifying glass.

"It's all before us!" said the crocodile.

"Every day!" said the spinster mouse editor.

"Ting-tang, tantarang!" sang the marching brass legs of the clock's escapement, and they all followed him out through the window and into the moonlight. Last of all was whoever lived in the red-and-yellow glass-topped box that had been the monkey game of skill.

"They'll want me too," he said. "Everyone can't be nice."